Chels-
I know its Christmas but
you aren't going to be around
in Feb. So
will you be my
Valentine?
Please?
Pretty Please?

-Bryan

# Little Mouse's Big Valentine

FOR OLIVIA

## by Thacher Hurd

HarperCollins*Publishers*

Library of Congress Cataloging-in-Publication Data
Hurd, Thacher.
    Little Mouse's big valentine / by Thacher Hurd.
        p.      cm.
    Summary: After several unsuccessful attempts to give his special valentine to
someone, Little Mouse finally finds just the right recipient.
    ISBN 0-06-026192-7.—ISBN 0-06-026193-5 (lib. bdg.)
    [1. Mice—Fiction.   2. Valentines—Fiction.]   I. Title.
PZ7.H9562Li   1990                                                    89-34515
[E]—dc20                                                                    CIP
                                                                              AC

One morning, Little Mouse took out
a jar of red paint,
a big piece of paper,
and a pair of scissors.
Then he made a valentine.

But Little Mouse's valentine was so big

that nobody wanted it.

Squirrel said, "Where would I hide it?"

Mole said, "It's too bright. It hurts my eyes."

Woodchuck said, "I already have a valentine."

Owl said, "It looks silly to me."

So Little Mouse went looking for someone else
to give his valentine to.

Little Mouse walked until he came to
a river. He stood at the edge of the water
and called out, "Who would like a great big
valentine?"

But the fish in the river just swam on.

Little Mouse paddled his valentine
across the river.

On the other side there was a big hill.
Little Mouse started to climb the hill.
His valentine was heavy.

At last, Little Mouse came to the top of the hill.
He sat down to rest.
Suddenly, a hawk swooped down out of the sky
and grabbed the big valentine.

Little Mouse held on tight.

Up, up, up went the hawk.
Little Mouse looked down.
It was a long way down.

Just then, the hawk let go of the valentine.
Little Mouse tumbled down.

Luckily, Little Mouse found
he could steer the big valentine.

Little Mouse steered his valentine through some trees
and landed on a pile of leaves.
Little Mouse heard a voice.

"Who are you?" said Little Mouse.
"I'm Gloria," said the other little mouse.
"What's that?"
"It's a valentine," said Little Mouse.
"I'm looking for someone to give it to."

"I'll help you carry it," said Gloria.
"Perhaps together we can find someone to give it to."
The two little mice carried the valentine together.
Soon Gloria said, "I'm getting a little tired."
"So am I," said Little Mouse.

"Look," said Gloria. "There is my house."
"It looks like a nice house," said Little Mouse.

Gloria and Little Mouse leaned the big valentine
against Gloria's house.
Then they sat on the lawn and ate a snack.
Little Mouse smiled at Gloria.
Gloria smiled at Little Mouse.

They held paws.
"I have been thinking," said Little Mouse.
"Oh," said Gloria.
"I have been thinking that I would like to give
my big valentine to you," said Little Mouse.
"But it *is* awfully big," said Gloria.

Little Mouse sat and thought.
He asked Gloria, "Do you have two pairs of scissors?"
Gloria went into her house and rummaged around.
"Yes," she called out, and she brought them outside.
Then, out of that one big valentine,
Little Mouse and Gloria made

Valentines for everyone....

And the nicest one was for Gloria.